big&SMALL

Original Korean text by Seon-hye Jang
Illustrations by Hyeong-jin Lee
Korean edition © Aram Publishing

This English edition published by big & SMALL in 2017
by arrangement with Aram Publishing
English text edited by Joy Cowley
English edition © big & SMALL 2017

Distributed in the United States and Canada by
Lerner Publishing Group, Inc.
241 First Avenue North
Minneapolis, MN 55401 U.S.A.
www.lernerbooks.com

ISBN: 978-1-925234-83-1

Printed in Korea

Animal Talk

Written by Seon-hye Jang
Illustrated by Hyeong-jin Lee
Edited by Joy Cowley

People and animals
say things in different ways.

Elephants don't give flowers
to say, "I like you."

Elephant

Elephants say "I like you" with their trunks.

They make a good pair!

Ants

These birds say
"I like you"
with a dance.

Blue-footed booby

Peacock

This bird shows off
its feathers.

10

This frog sings loud songs
to find a mate.

Female frog

Male frog

11

A rhinoceros doesn't need a fence
to keep other animals out.

13

A rhinoceros marks its territory with its dung.

Rhinoceros

14

15

A bear makes claw marks
on trees to mark its territory.

Brown bear

16

Lark

A lark marks its territory
with its song.

A deer marks its territory
with a scent.

Deer

17

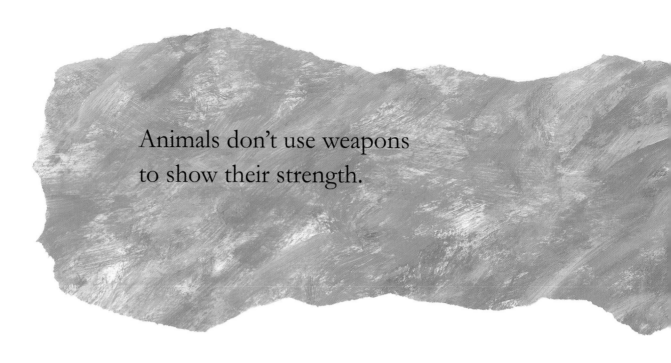

Animals don't use weapons
to show their strength.

18

A hippopotamus uses its mouth.

Hippopotamus

Turtle

They're always fighting!

Giraffe

Giraffes fight
with their long necks.

Camel

Balancing on their tails, kangaroos fight with their front feet.

Kangaroo

Camels spit when they are angry.

23

When animals lose a fight,
this is what they do...

Cow

A cow will run away!

Cow

Duck

Running away?
See you later!

Dog

A dog rolls on its back
and shows its belly.

28

Shimofuri goby fish

You win!
See my two stripes?

A wolf puts its ears down
and lies flat on the ground.

Wolf

Animals communicate with each other
in many different ways.
They can say "hello" to friends
with their dung.
They can warn friends of danger
by showing their white tails.

White-tailed deer

Raccoon

Animal Talk

Animals don't talk to each other in the same way that people do. They don't use words. Animals use their senses to communicate. They send messages by leaving scents, making loud calls, showing their feathers, and fighting with different parts of their bodies. Let's learn about the different ways animals communicate.

Let's think!

How does a frog find a mate?

How does a rhinoceros mark its territory?

What does a camel do when it is angry?

What happens when a cow loses a fight?

Let's do!

Try to communicate with your friends without using words. Play charades. Write down some different animal names or actions on pieces of paper. Put the papers in a jar. Pull out a paper, read it, and act it out without using any words. See how fast your friends can guess what you are trying to communicate!